Vasilisa the Beautiful

and Baba Yaga

Recorded by
Alexander Afanasyev

Illustrations by Ivan Bilibin

Vasilisa the Beautiful and Baba Yaga by Alexander Afanasyev

Illustrations by Ivan Bilibin

Translation by Post Wheeler

ISBN 978-1-916581-14-2

Published by The Planet, 2023

www.the-planet-books.com

1899

2023

Illustrations by Ivan Bilibin

VASILISA THE BEAUTIFUL

Many years ago, in a certain Tsardom, across three times nine kingdoms, beyond high mountain chains, there once lived a merchant. He had been married for twelve years, but in that time there had been born to him only one child, a daughter, who from her cradle was called Vasilisa the Beautiful. When the little girl was eight years old, her mother fell ill, and before many days it was plain to be seen that she must die. So she called her little daughter to her, took a tiny wooden doll from under the blanket of the bed, put it into her hands and said: "My little Vasilisa, my dear daughter, listen to what I say, remember well my last words and fail not to carry out my wishes. I am dying, and with my blessing, I leave to thee this little doll. It is very precious, for there is no other like it in the whole world. Carry it always about with thee in thy pocket and never show it to anyone. When evil threatens thee or sorrow befalls thee, go into a corner, take it from thy pocket and give it something to eat and drink. It will eat and drink a little, and then thou mayest tell it thy trouble and ask its advice, and it will tell thee how to act in thy time of need." So saying, she kissed her little daughter on the forehead, blessed her, and shortly after died.

Little Vasilisa grieved greatly for her mother, and her sorrow was so deep that when the dark night came, she lay in her bed and wept and did not sleep. At length she bethought herself of the tiny doll, so she rose and took it from the pocket of her gown, and finding a piece of wheat bread and a cup of kvass, she set them before it and said: "There, my little doll, take it. Eat a little, and drink a little, and listen to my grief. My dear mother is dead, and I am lonely for her."

Then the doll's eyes began to shine like fireflies, and suddenly it became alive. It ate a morsel of the bread and took a sip of the kvass, and when it had eaten and drank, it said: "Don't weep, little Vasilisa. Grief is worst at night. Lie down, shut thine eyes, comfort thyself and go to sleep. The morning is wiser than the evening." So Vasilisa the Beautiful lay down, comforted herself and went to sleep, and the next day her grieving was not so deep and her tears were less bitter.

Now after the death of his wife, the merchant sorrowed for many days as was right, but at the end of that time he began to desire to marry again and to look about him for a suitable wife. This was not difficult to find, for he had a fine house with a stable of swift horses, besides being a good man who gave much to the poor. Of all the

8

women he saw, however, the one who, to his mind, suited him best of all, was a widow of about his own age with two daughters of her own, and she, he thought, besides being a good housekeeper, would be a kind foster mother to his little Vasilisa.

So the merchant married the widow and brought her home as his wife, but the little girl soon found that her foster mother was very far from being what her father had thought. She was a cold, cruel woman, who had desired the merchant for the sake of his wealth, and had no love for his daughter. Vasilisa was the greatest beauty in the whole village, while the daughters of the foster mother were as spare and homely as two crows, and because of this all three envied and hated Vasilisa. They gave her all sorts of errands to run and difficult tasks to perform, in order that the toil might make her thin and worn, and that her face might grow brown from sun and wind; and they treated her so cruelly as to leave few joys in life for her. But little Vasilisa endured all this without complaint, and while the stepmother's two daughters grew always thinner and uglier in spite of the fact that they had no hard tasks to do, never went out in cold or rain, and sat always with their arms folded like ladies of a Court, she herself had cheeks like blood and milk and grew every day more and more beautiful.

Now the reason for this was the tiny doll, without whose help little Vasilisa could never have managed to do all the work that was laid upon her. Each night, when everyone else was sound asleep, she would get up from her bed, take the doll into a closet, and locking the door, give it something to eat and drink, and say: "There, my little doll, take it. Eat a little, drink a little, and listen to my grief. I live in my father's house, but my spiteful stepmother wishes to drive me out of the white world. Tell me! How shall I act, and what shall I do?"

Then the little doll's eyes would begin to shine like glowworms, and it would become alive. It would eat a little food and sip a little drink, and then it would comfort her and tell her how to act. While Vasilisa slept, it would get ready all her work for the next day, so that she had only to rest in the shade and gather flowers, for the doll would have the kitchen garden weeded, and the beds of cabbage watered, and plenty of fresh water brought from the well, and the stoves heated exactly right. And, besides this, the little doll told her how to make, from a certain herb, an ointment which prevented her from ever being sunburnt. So all the joy in life that came to Vasilisa came to her through the tiny doll that she always carried in her pocket.

Years passed, till Vasilisa grew up and became of an age when it is good to marry. All the young men in the village, high and low, rich and poor, asked for her hand, while not one of them stopped even to look at the stepmother's two daughters, so ill-favoured were they. This angered their mother still more against Vasilisa; she answered every gallant who came with the same words: "Never shall the younger be wed before the older ones!" and each time, when she had let a suitor out of the door, she would soothe her anger and hatred by beating her stepdaughter. So while Vasilisa grew each day more lovely and graceful, she was often miserable, and but for the little doll in her pocket, would have longed to leave the white world.

Now there came a time when it became necessary for the merchant to leave his home and to travel to a distant Tsardom. He bade farewell to his wife and her two daughters, kissed Vasilisa and gave her his blessing and departed, bidding them say a prayer each day for his safe return. Scarce was he out of sight of the village, however, when his wife sold his house, packed all his goods and moved with them to another dwelling far from the town, in a gloomy neighbourhood on the edge of a wild forest. Here, every day, while her two daughters were working indoors, the merchant's wife would send Vasilisa on one errand or other into the forest, either to find a branch of a certain rare bush or to bring her flowers or berries.

Now deep in this forest, as the stepmother well knew, there was a green lawn, and on the lawn stood a little hut on hens' legs, where lived a certain Baba Yaga, an old witch grandmother. She lived alone, and none dared go near the hut, for she ate people as one eats chickens. The merchant's wife sent Vasilisa into the forest each day, hoping she might meet the old witch and be devoured; but always the girl came home safe and sound, because the little doll showed her where the bush, the flowers and the berries grew, and did not let her go near the hut that stood on hens' legs. And each time the stepmother hated her more and more because she came to no harm.

One autumn evening the merchant's wife called the three girls to her and gave them each a task. One of her daughters she bade make a piece of lace, the other to knit a pair of hose, and to Vasilisa she gave a basket of flax to be spun. She bade each finish a certain amount. Then she put out all the fires in the house, leaving only a single candle lighted in the room where the three girls worked, and she herself went to sleep.

They worked an hour, they worked two hours, they worked three hours, when one of the elder daughters took up the tongs to straighten the wick of the candle. She pretended to do this awkwardly (as her mother had bidden her) and put the candle out, as if by accident.

"What are we to do now?" asked her sister. "The fires are all out, there is no other light in all the house, and our tasks are not done."

"We must go and fetch fire," said the first. "The only house near is a hut in the forest, where a Baba Yaga lives. One of us must go and borrow fire from her."

"I have enough light from my steel pins," said the one who was making the lace, "and I will not go."

"And I have plenty of light from my silver needles," said the other, who was knitting the hose, "and I will not go."

"Thou, Vasilisa," they both said, "shalt go and fetch the fire, for thou hast neither steel pins nor silver needles and cannot see to spin thy flax!" They both rose up, pushed Vasilisa out of the house and locked the door, crying: "Thou shalt not come in till thou hast fetched the fire."

Vasilisa sat down on the doorstep, took the tiny doll from one pocket and from another the supper she had ready for it, put the food before it and said: "There, my little doll, take it. Eat a little and listen to my sorrow. I must go to the hut of the old Baba Yaga in the dark forest to borrow some fire, and I fear she will eat me. Tell me! What shall I do?"

Then the doll's eyes began to shine like two stars, and it became alive. It ate a little and said: "Do not fear, little Vasilisa. Go where thou hast been sent. While I am with thee, no harm shall come to thee from the old witch." So Vasilisa put the doll back into her pocket, crossed herself and started out into the dark, wild forest.

Whether she walked a short way or a long way, the telling is easy, but the journey was hard. The wood was very dark, and she could not help trembling from fear. Suddenly she heard the sound of a horse's hoofs, and a man on horseback galloped past her. He was dressed all in white, the horse under him was milk-white, and the harness was white; and just as he passed her, it became twilight.

She went a little further, and again she heard the sound of a horse's hoofs, and there came another man on horseback galloping past her. He was dressed all in red, and the horse under him was blood-red,

and its harness was red; and just as he passed her, the sun rose.

That whole day Vasilisa walked, for she had lost her way. She could find no path at all in the dark wood, and she had no food to set before the little doll to make it alive.

But at evening she came all at once to the green lawn where the wretched little hut stood on its hens' legs. The wall around the hut was made of human bones, and on its top were skulls. There was a gate in the wall, whose hinges were the bones of human feet and whose locks were jaw bones set with sharp teeth. The sight filled Vasilisa with horror, and she stopped as still as a post buried in the ground.

As she stood there, a third man on horseback came galloping up. His face was black, he was dressed all in black, and the horse he rode was coal-black. He galloped up to the gate of the hut and disappeared there as if he had sunk through the ground; and at that moment the night came, and the forest grew dark.

But it was not dark on the green lawn, for instantly the eyes of all the skulls on the wall were lighted up and shone till the place was as bright as day. Seeing this, Vasilisa trembled with fear so that she could not run away.

Then suddenly the wood became full of a terrible noise; the trees began to groan, the branches to creak and the dry leaves to rustle; and the Baba Yaga came flying from the forest. She was riding in a great iron mortar and driving it with a pestle; and she swept away the trail behind her with a kitchen broom.

She rode up to the gate and, stopping, said:

> "Little Hut, little Hut,
> "Stand the way thy mother placed thee,
> "Turn thy back to the forest and thy face to me!"

And the little hut turned facing her and stood still. Then smelling all around her, she cried: "Foo! Foo! I smell a smell that is Russian. Who is here?"

Vasilisa, in great fright, came nearer to the old woman and, bowing very low, said: "It is only Vasilisa, grandmother. My stepmother's daughters sent me to thee to borrow some fire."

"Well," said the old witch, "I know them. But if I give thee the fire, thou shalt stay with me some time and do some work to pay for it. If not, thou shalt be eaten for my supper." Then she turned to the gate and shouted: "Ho! ye, my solid locks, unlock! Thou, my stout gate, open!" Instantly the locks unlocked, the gate opened of itself, and the Baba Yaga rode in whistling. Vasilisa entered behind her, and immediately the gate shut again and the locks snapped tight.

When they had entered the hut, the old witch threw herself down on the stove, stretched out her bony legs and said: "Come, fetch and put on the table at once everything that is in the oven. I am hungry." So Vasilisa ran and lighted a splinter of wood from one of the skulls on the wall and took the food from the oven and set it before her. There was enough cooked meat for three strong men. She brought also from the cellar kvass, honey, beer and wine; and the Baba Yaga ate and drank the whole, leaving the girl only a little of cabbage soup, a crust of bread and a morsel of sucking pig.

When her hunger was satisfied, the old witch, growing drowsy, lay down on the stove and said: "Listen to me well and do what I bid thee. Tomorrow when I drive away, do thou clean the yard, sweep the floors and cook my supper. Then take a quarter of a measure of wheat from my storehouse and pick out of it all the black grains and the wild peas. Mind thou dost all that I have bade; if not, thou shalt be eaten for my supper."

Presently the Baba Yaga turned toward the wall and began to snore, and Vasilisa knew that she was fast asleep. Then she went into the corner, took the tiny doll from her pocket, put before it a bit of bread and a little cabbage soup that she had saved, burst into tears and said: "There, my little doll, take it. Eat a little, drink a little, and listen to my grief. Here I am in the house of the old witch, and the gate in the wall is locked, and I am afraid. She has given me a difficult task, and if I do not do all she has bade, she will eat me tomorrow. Tell me: what shall I do? "

Then the eyes of the little doll began to shine, like two candles. It ate a little of the bread and drank a little of the soup and said: "Don't be afraid, Vasilisa the Beautiful. Be comforted. Say thy prayers and go to sleep. The morning is wiser than the evening." So Vasilisa trusted the little doll and was comforted. She said her prayers, lay down on the floor and went fast asleep.

When she woke next morning, very early, it was still dark. She rose and looked out of the window, and she saw that the eyes of the skulls on the wall were growing dim. As she looked, the man dressed all in white, riding the milk-white horse, galloped swiftly around the corner of the hut, leaped the wall and disappeared; and as he went, it became quite light and the eyes of the skulls flickered and went out. The old witch was in the yard; now she began to whistle, and the great iron mortar and pestle and the kitchen broom flew out of the hut to her. As she got into the mortar, the man dressed all in red mounted on the blood-red horse, galloped like the wind around the corner of the hut, leaped the wall and was gone; and at that moment the sun rose. Then the Baba Yaga shouted: "Ho! ye, my solid locks, unlock! Thou, my stout gate, open!" The locks unlocked and the gate opened, and she rode away in the mortar, driving with the pestle and sweeping away the trail behind her with the broom.

When Vasilisa found herself left alone, she examined the hut, wondering to find it filled with such an abundance of everything. Then she stood still, remembering all the work that she had been bidden to do and wondering what to begin first. But as she looked, she rubbed her eyes: the yard was already neatly cleaned and the floors were nicely swept, and the little doll was sitting in the store-house picking the last black grains and wild peas out of the quarter measure of wheat.

Vasilisa ran and took the little doll in her arms. "My dearest little doll!" she cried. "Thou hast saved me from my trouble! Now I have only to cook the Baba Yaga's supper, since all the rest of the tasks are done!"

"Cook it, with God's help," said the doll, "and then rest, and may the cooking of it make you healthy!" And so saying it crept into her pocket and became again only a little wooden doll.

So Vasilisa rested all day and was refreshed; and when it grew toward evening, she laid the table for the old witch's supper and sat looking out of the window, waiting for her coming. After awhile she heard the sound of horse's hoofs, and the man in black, on the coal-black horse, galloped up to the wall gate and disappeared like a great dark shadow; and instantly it became quite dark, and the eyes of all the skulls began to glitter and shine.

Then all at once the trees of the forest began to creak and groan, and the leaves and the bushes to moan and sigh; and the Baba Yaga came riding out of the dark wood in the huge iron mortar, driving with the pestle and sweeping out the trail behind her with the kitchen broom. Vasilisa let her in, and the witch, smelling all around her, asked:

"Well, hast thou done perfectly all the tasks I gave thee to do, or am I to eat thee for my supper?"

"Be so good as to look for thyself, grandmother," answered Vasilisa.

The Baba Yaga went all about the place, tapping with her iron pestle, and carefully examining everything. But so well had the little doll done its work that, try as hard as she might, the old witch could not find anything to complain of. There was not a weed left in the yard, nor a speck of dust on the floors, nor a single black grain or wild pea in the wheat.

She was greatly angered, but was obliged to pretend to be pleased. "Well," she said, "thou hast done all well." Then, clapping her hands, she shouted: "Ho! my faithful servants! Friends of my heart! Haste and grind my wheat!" Immediately three pairs of hands appeared, seized the measure of wheat and carried it away.

The Baba Yaga sat down to supper, and Vasilisa put before her all the food from the oven, with kvass, honey, beer and wine. The old witch ate it, bones and all, almost to the last morsel, enough for four strong men, and then, growing drowsy, stretched her bony legs on the stove and said: "Tomorrow do as thou hast done today, and besides these tasks take from my storehouse a half-measure of poppy seeds and clean them one by one. Someone has mixed earth with them to do me a mischief and to anger me, and I will have them made perfectly clean." So saying she turned to the wall and soon began to snore.

When she was fast asleep, Vasilisa went into the corner, took the little doll from her pocket, set before it a part of the food that was left and asked its advice. And the doll, when it had become alive and eaten a little food and sipped a little drink, said: "Don't worry, beautiful Vasilisa! Be comforted. Do as thou didst last night: say thy prayers and go to sleep." So Vasilisa was comforted. She said her prayers and went to sleep and did not wake till next morning when she heard the old witch in the yard whistling. She ran to the window just in time to see her take her place in the big iron mortar; and as she did so, the man dressed all in red, riding on the blood-red horse, leaped over the wall and was gone, just as the sun rose over the wild forest.

As it had happened on the first morning, so it happened now. When Vasilisa looked, she found that the little doll had finished all the tasks except the cooking of the supper. The yard was swept and in order, the floors were as clean as new wood, and there was not a grain of earth left in the half-measure of poppy seeds. She rested and refreshed herself till the afternoon when she cooked the supper;

and when evening came, she laid the table and sat down to wait for the old witch's coming.

Soon the man in black, on the coal-black horse, galloped up to the gate, and the dark fell, and the eyes of the skulls began to shine like day; then the ground began to quake, and the trees of the forest began to creak, and the dry leaves to rustle, and the Baba Yaga came riding in her iron mortar, driving with her pestle and sweeping away her trail with her broom.

When she came in, she smelled around her and went all about the hut, tapping with the pestle; but pry and examine as she might, again she could see no reason to find fault and was angrier than ever.

She clapped her hands and shouted: "Ho! my trusty servants! Friends of my soul! Haste and press the oil out of my poppy seeds!"

And instantly the three pairs of hands appeared, seized the measure of poppy seeds and carried it away.

Presently the old witch sat down to supper, and Vasilisa brought all she had cooked, enough for five grown men, and set it before her, and brought beer and honey; and then she herself stood silently waiting. The Baba Yaga ate and drank it all, every morsel, leaving not so much as a crumb of bread; then she said snappishly: "Well, why dost thou say nothing, but stand there as if thou wast dumb?"

"I spoke not," Vasilisa answered, "because I dared not. But if thou wilt allow me, grandmother, I wish to ask thee some questions."

"Well," said the old witch, "only remember that every question does not lead to good. If thou knowest overmuch, thou wilt grow old too soon. What wilt thou ask?"

"I would ask thee," said Vasilisa, "of the men on horseback. When I came to thy hut, a rider passed me. He was dressed all in white, and he rode a milk-white horse. Who was he?"

"That was my white, bright day," answered the Baba Yaga angrily. "He is a servant of mine, but he cannot hurt thee. Ask me more."

"Afterwards," said Vasilisa, "a second rider overtook me. He was dressed in red, and the horse he rode was blood-red. Who was he?"

"That was my servant, the round, red sun," answered the Baba Yaga, "and he, too, cannot injure thee," and she ground her teeth. "Ask me more."

"A third rider," said Vasilisa, "came galloping up to the gate. He was black, his clothes were black, and the horse was coal-black. Who was he?"

"That was my servant, the black, dark night," answered the old witch furiously; "but he also cannot harm thee. Ask me more."

But Vasilisa, remembering what the Baba Yaga had said, that not every question led to good, was silent.

"Ask me more!" cried the old witch. "Why dost thou not ask me more? Ask me of the three pairs of hands that serve me!"

But Vasilisa saw how she snarled at her and she answered: "The three questions are enough for me. As thou hast said, grandmother, I would not, through knowing over much, become too soon old."

"It is well for thee," said the Baba Yaga, "that thou didst not ask of them, but only of what thou didst see outside of this hut. Hadst thou asked of them, my servants, the three pairs of hands would have seized thee also, as they did the wheat and poppy seeds, to be my food. Now I would ask a question in my turn: How is it that thou hast been able, in a little time, to do perfectly all the tasks I gave thee? Tell me!"

Vasilisa was so frightened to see how the old witch ground her teeth that she almost told her of the little doll; but she bethought herself just in time and answered: "The blessing of my dead mother helps me."

Then the Baba Yaga sprang up in a fury. "Get thee out of my house this moment!" she shrieked. "I want no one who bears a blessing to cross my threshold! Get thee gone!"

Vasilisa ran to the yard, and behind her she heard the old witch shouting to the locks and the gate. The locks opened, the gate swung wide, and she ran out on to the lawn. The Baba Yaga seized from the wall one of the skulls with burning eyes and flung it after her. "There," she howled, "is the fire for thy stepmother's daughters. Take it. That is what they sent thee here for, and may they have joy of it!"

Vasilisa put the skull on the end of a stick and darted away through the forest, running as fast as she could, finding her path by the skull's glowing eyes, which went out only when morning came.

Whether she ran a long way or a short way, and whether the road was smooth or rough, towards evening of the next day, when the eyes in the skull were beginning to glimmer, she came out of the dark, wild forest to her stepmother's house.

When she came near to the gate, she thought, "Surely, by this time they will have found some fire," and threw the skull into the hedge; but it spoke to her and said: "Do not throw me away, beautiful Vasilisa; bring me to thy stepmother." So, looking at the house and seeing no spark of light in any of the windows, she took up the skull again and carried it with her.

Now since Vasilisa had gone, the stepmother and her two daughters had had neither fire nor light in all the house. When they struck flint and steel, the tinder would not catch, and the fire they brought from the neighbours would go out immediately as soon as they carried it over the threshold, so that they had been unable to light or warm themselves or to cook food to eat. Therefore now, for the first

time in her life, Vasilisa found herself welcomed. They opened the door to her, and the merchant's wife was greatly rejoiced to find that the light in the skull did not go out as soon as it was brought in. "Maybe the witch's fire will stay," she said, took the skull into the best room, set it on a candlestick and called her two daughters to admire it.

But the eyes of the skull suddenly began to glimmer and to glow like red coals, and wherever the three turned or ran, the eyes followed them, growing larger and brighter till they flamed like two furnaces, and hotter and hotter till the merchant's wife and her two wicked daughters took fire and were burned to ashes. Only Vasilisa the Beautiful was not touched.

In the morning Vasilisa dug a deep hole in the ground and buried the skull. Then she locked the house and set out to the village, where she went to live with an old woman who was poor and childless; and so she remained for many days, waiting for her father's return from the far-distant kingdom.

But, sitting lonely, time soon began to hang heavy on her hands. One day she said to the old woman: "It is dull for me, grandmother, to sit idly hour by hour. My hands want work to do. Go, therefore, and buy me some flax, the best and finest to be found anywhere, and at least I can spin."

The old woman hastened and bought some flax of the best sort, and Vasilisa sat down to work. So well did she spin that the thread came out as even and fine as a hair, and presently there was enough to begin to weave. But so fine was the thread that no frame could be found to weave it upon, nor would any weaver undertake to make one.

Then Vasilisa went into her closet, took the little doll from her pocket, set food and drink before it and asked its help. And after it had eaten a little and drunk a little, the doll became alive and said: "Bring me an old frame and an old basket and some hairs from a horse's mane, and I will arrange everything for thee." Vasilisa hastened to fetch all the doll had asked for, and when evening came, she said her prayers, went to sleep, and in the morning she found ready a frame, perfectly made, to weave her fine thread upon.

She wove one month, she wove two months—all the winter Vasilisa sat weaving, weaving her fine thread, till the whole piece of linen was done, of a texture so fine that it could be passed, like thread, through the eye of a needle. When the spring came, she bleached it, so white that no snow could be compared with it. Then she said to the old woman: "Take thou the linen to the market, grandmother, and sell it, and the money shall suffice to pay for my food and lodging." When the old woman had examined the linen, however, she said: "Never will I sell such cloth in the marketplace; no one should wear it except it be the Tsar himself, and tomorrow I shall carry it to the Palace."

Next day, accordingly, the old woman went to the Tsar's splendid Palace and fell to walking up and down before the windows. The servants came to ask her her errand but she answered them nothing, and kept walking up and down. At length the Tsar opened his window and asked: "What dost thou want, old woman, that thou walkest here?"

"O Tsar's Majesty!" the old woman answered, "I have with me a marvellous piece of linen stuff, so wondrously woven that I will show it to none but thee."

The Tsar bade them bring her before him, and when he saw the linen, he was struck with astonishment at its fineness and beauty. "What wilt thou take for it, old woman?" he asked.

"There is no price that can buy it, our Father Tsar," she answered; "but I have brought it to thee as a gift."

The Tsar could not thank the old woman enough. He took the linen and sent her to her house with many rich presents.

Seamstresses were called to make shirts for him out of the cloth; but when it had been cut up, so fine was it that no one of them was deft and skillful enough to sew it. The best seamstresses in all the Tsardom were summoned but none dared undertake it. So at last the Tsar sent for the old woman and said: "If thou didst know how to spin such thread and weave such linen, thou must also know how to sew me shirts from it."

And the old woman answered: "O Tsar's Majesty, it was not I who wove the linen; it is the work of my adopted daughter."

"Take it, then," the Tsar said, "and bid her do it for me."

The old woman brought the linen home and told Vasilisa the Tsar's command: "Well, I knew that the work would needs be done by my own hands," said Vasilisa, and, locking herself in her own room, began to make the shirts. So fast and well did she work that soon a dozen were ready. Then the old woman carried them to the Tsar, while Vasilisa washed her face, dressed her hair, put on her best gown and sat down at the window to see what would happen. And presently a servant in the livery of the Palace came to the house and said: "The Tsar, our lord, desires himself to see the clever needlewoman who has made his shirts and to reward her with his own hands."

Vasilisa rose and went at once to the Palace, and as soon as the Tsar saw her, he fell in love with her with all his soul. He took her by her white hand and made her sit beside him. "Beautiful maiden," he said, "never will I part from thee, and thou shalt be my wife."

So the Tsar and Vasilisa the Beautiful were married, and her father returned from the far distant kingdom, and he and the old

woman lived always with her in the splendid Palace, in all joy and contentment. And as for the little wooden doll, Vasilisa carried it about with her in her pocket all her life long.

Made in the USA
Monee, IL
28 January 2024

52549303R00019